characters created by

lauren chil

I'm really really ever so NOT well

PUFFIN

Charlie ♥ and ♥ Lola™

Text based on the script written by Dave Ingham

Illustrations from the TV animation produced by Tiger Aspect

PUFFIN BOOKS
Published by the Penguin Group: London, New York, Australia,
Canada, India, Ireland, New Zealand and South Africa
Penguin Books Ltd, Registered Offices: 80 Strand, London WC2R 0RL, England

puffinbooks.com

First published 2007
Published in this edition 2008
1 3 5 7 9 10 8 6 4 2
Text and illustrations copyright © Lauren Child/Tiger Aspect Productions Limited, 2007
The Charlie and Lola logo is a trademark of Lauren Child
Made and printed in China
ISBN: 978-0-141-50081-2

I have this little sister Lola.
She is small and very funny.
Well, usually she's very funny,
but not when she's not feeling very well.
And today Lola's really not feeling well.

Lola has a cold.

I say, "How are you feeling, Lola?"

Lola says,
"I'm really, really
     ever so **not well**,
                Charlie."

So I say,
"Mum's given me some pink
milk and biscuits for you, Lola."

Pink milk is Lola's favourite.

But Lola says,

"Yuck!
My pink milk
tastes green.

And the biscuits
are too prickly
to swallow.

I don't feel like
eating or drinking
anything."

Then Lola says, "I remember when everything tasted yummy..."

So I say,
"Dad always says flowers are very good
at cheering little people up."

But Lola says,

"Aaaachooooooooo!

Get
Well SOON!

They're not very good at
cheering up this little person!"

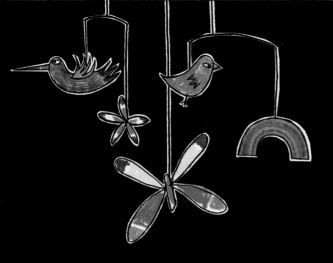

Then Lola says,
"My **n**°**se** hurts,
and nothing **smells**.

I remember when I used to be able to do **smelling**....

Then I have an **idea** how to **cheer** up Lola.

I say, "I know...
let's sing a **SONG**."

But Lola says,
"I can't do **singing**, Charlie...
my **throat** hurts and
my voice is all quiet."

Then she says,
"I remember singing...

'The sun has
got his hat on,

Hip, hip, hip
hooray,

The sun
has got
his hat on

and he's
coming
out
today!'"

Lola says,
    "Can **you** sing for me, Charlie?"

    I say,
"I can't. I've got a big football game
        and I've promised Marv I'll play.
I can't break my promise."

Let's **sing** a **Song!**

"Pleeease, Charlie,"
says Lola.

So I say,
"All right then...

'If you're happy

and you know it

clap

your

hands...

Then I say,
"You're not clapping, Lola."

"I'm not happy, Charlie," says Lola.
"Why do I feel so really, really not well?"

So I say, "It's those germs in your mouth."

"Germs?"
says Lola.

And I say,
"Your cold germs. Would you
like to see them, Lola?"

So I take Lola
to the bathroom
to look in the mirror.

Say "Ahhhhh!"

Lola says,

"Ahhhhhhhhhhh..."

Then I hear the phone ringing.
I say,
"It's probably Marv.
I'd better go and answer it."

Marv says,
"So, are you coming
to play football then?
It's a big game, you know!"

I say,
"Yes, it's just that Lola..."

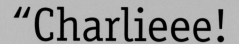

"Charlieee!
I feel really, really
terribly **ever so**
NOT well,"
says Lola.

And I say,
"I've just told Marv that
        I'm on my way. Mum says
she'll come and play with you."

And Lola says,
    "But I want you
to play with me, Charlie!"

    So I say, "Okay.
How about a quick jigsaw puzzle?"

The **smiley** puzzle is Lola's **favourite**.

Then I hear the phone ringing again and I know it's going to be Marv...

Marv says,
"So you're definitely
coming then?"

I say,
"Of course I am...
I'm coming...
right now!"

Lola says,
"Charlie! I want you
to stay...

Please?"

And then I have a really good idea.
"Hey, Lola," I say.
"Where's your butterfly gone...?"

"To Flutterby Mountain!" says Lola.

"Yes," I say.
"Do you want to try and catch him?"

Lola says, "I love cloud hopping, Charlie."

Hip, hip, hip hooray!

"Come on, Charlie!"
says Marv.

And I say,
"All ri...

Ah...

Ah...

Ah...

The next day, I'm in bed feeling really not well.
        Lola says, "So, how are you feeling, Charlie?"

I say,
"I'm really... really
     not well, Lola!"

And Lola says,
      "Don't worry,
           Charlie...

           ...because I'm going to be here every
      minute of all day until you're
                 completely absolutely **better!**"

And I say,
"Every minute of all day...
Muuummm!"

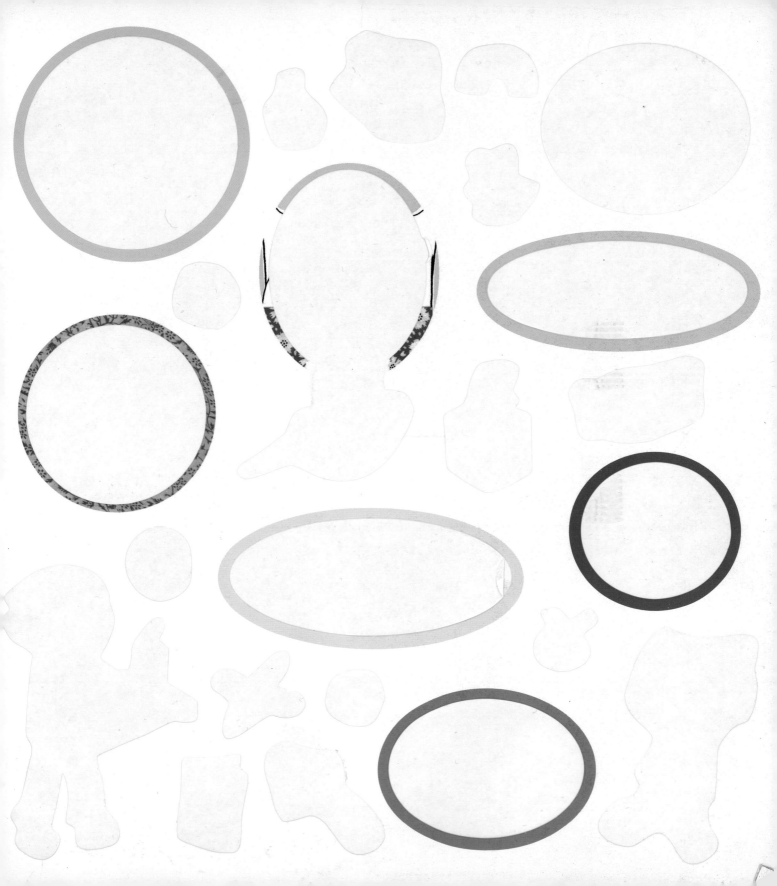

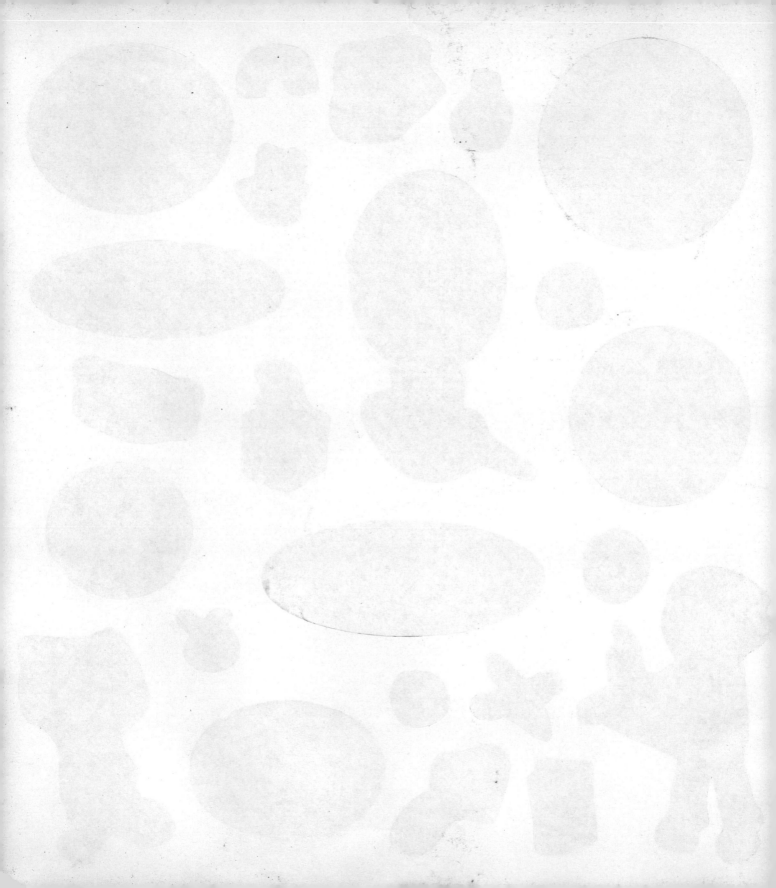